Lexi's Triplets

Book One

Jean Lee

DEDICATION

Lexi's Triplets is dedicated to

Hunter, Ava, Maxwell, their parents

and of course, Lexi.

Being included in your lives has been one of Gray Granny's greatest joys.

MARCH 13

Help!

I have to vent! Bark out!

My name is Lexi Lee and I'm stressed beyond the point of nervous licking. I need support before I start chewing shoes or worse—the couch cushions.

I'm lonely.

It's 4:00 a.m. I'm stuck, with no one to talk to. I've tried heart-to-hearts with Riley Cat, but she's not spoken to me in the five years since Mom and Dad brought me home, except to hiss and bat in a jealous rage.

I'm desperate.

Tonight, in a rare moment when everyone was asleep, I snuck out of Mom and Dad's bed, not an easy thing to do at 70-pounds of big-buttedness.

Reaching with my front paws, I planned to jump my hindquarters down, but couldn't risk the noise. At the last moment I turned and slid my bottom half to the floor, reaching with tippy-toes, holding my breath hoping the bed wouldn't squeak. I'd be in huge trouble if I woke anyone.

I padded past Gray Granny, shut behind the guestroom door.

She doesn't like me. I wish she'd go home.

The sound of her snoring drowned out the creaking stairway and my uncontrollable, banging tail.

I braved my way down the basement steps gritty with cat litter. I hate the basement as much as Riley Cat hates me.

Since we fight like cats and dogs, I'm forced to find cyber doggie friends by building my own device from cords, cables, modems, and motherboards stolen from Dad's computer graveyard strewn about the cellar.

I'm spooked, afraid of being caught.

But, I can assemble, connect, upload a profile picture, and begin blogging in under an hour. Plus, I've claimed the empty space under an old desk as my work area, the bottom drawer perfectly sized for secret storage of my not-too-shabby doggy-built computer.

Now, let me circle round to tell you how my world began to crumble.

A few months back I, the beloved house pet, guarded our little castle while Mom and Dad went to work. I took my security job seriously, always on keen alert for the mail carrier and UPS deliveryman.

The guy in the brown uniform liked me so much he started leaving me Milkbones.

In between times I have to admit, the couch was my own and I napped, but those were the perks of a job well done.

After work, Dad played fetch and Frisbee with me in the fenced yard. On sunny evenings, Mom, Dad, and I grilled supper and ate among the roses.

Gradually I noticed Mom's belly growing. She stopped going to work and groaned each time she changed positions on the couch. She would cuddle me even when her stomach, stretched huge with so much writhing, seemed to kick me.

I didn't mind; we'd never been closer.

Grandma Strawberry and Gray Granny took turns staying, invading. They fretted every time Mom stood. Maybe they worried her belly would pull her off balance, or worse, burst.

All furniture was occupied with people. They shooed me off my own couch cushions. Grandma Strawberry and Gray Granny brought Mom things to eat, but forgot me. I had to beg, my hot breath panting on their knees. I was reduced to slobbering.

I've lost a couple of pounds. I think my vet would be pleased, but I'm terrified I could starve.

Two weeks ago, Dad helped Mom waddle out of the house, but only Dad returned. I panicked. Dad, Grandma, and Granny rushed in and out of the house at odd hours. No one spoke to me. I jumped and yipped to remind them to let me out as they hurried through. Once the door was closed with me stuck in the house, I paced. Nobody told me anything.

I choked back tears.

I missed Mom. Dad always wore a concerned scowl.

About a week ago I overheard the words "cesarean," "NICU," and the names, "Hunter," "Ava," and "Maxwell." Grandma Strawberry nicknamed the trio "HAMs."

I licked my chops, finally a good dinner.

Then last night, while I worry-wart-patrolled at the window, Dad's car pulled in the driveway. He stepped from the driver's door. Mom slowly scooted out of the passenger's side. I was overjoyed to see her. My heart thumping, I leaped and barked at the window.

Mom, Mom, why aren't you looking at me?

She and Dad didn't rush to greet me. Instead, they opened the doors of the backseat and removed three little padded chairs. When they pushed me aside to come in the front door, I saw a tiny, squirming, living being strapped into each seat.

O.M.G. have they brought me three hairless puppies to take care of? I'm already overworked.

TAKE THEM BACK.

I sniffed. They didn't smell like dogs.

Mom finally bent down to snuggle me and I realized her tummy wasn't big anymore. Did these creatures come out of her? They smelled human, but they were not even as long as my tail, and much lighter than the leather purse I chewed last Christmas.

Mom and Dad call these things "triplets."

Mom snapped this picture before taking the critters out of their seats.

Do I look petrified? Well, I am!

7

Mom and Dad seemed near tears too, wringing their hands as they stood looking down at the little ones.

As a bright spot in the chaos Gray Granny brought dinner—turkey, not ham—which Mom and Dad devoured while the itty ones slept in their seats. I was thrown a few scraps of stuffing. But, I couldn't eat. I've heard people say they feel sick as a dog. I don't understand what that means, but I felt sick as a human.

Oh, no, I hear whimpering and Mom and Dad's feet rushing around the kitchen upstairs. Cut short, that's all I have time to post tonight, or should I say this morning, since through the basement window, black night is tinged with gray dawn. I'd better traipse back upstairs, trying to quiet my nervous nails from clicking. I don't want Mom and Dad to get suspicious and find my computer. But some attention—even if I got scolded—would be better than none at all.

Before I log out, I've got to be honest, I'm worried. Am I being replaced?

Neither Riley Cat nor I came out of Mom's tummy. I tear up remembering the day I felt like the world's luckiest dog when Mom and Dad chose me out of the lineup at the animal shelter.

But now I can't shake the uneasy feeling I'm slipping a notch lower on the family food chain.

After all, here I am sitting in the basement with Riley who was downgraded when I replaced her. Now she skitters through a tiny cat door to and from the dungeon so she doesn't sneeze and cough up hairballs all over the place.

Thankfully, Mom and Dad don't have to put up with disgusting behaviors like that from me.

Mom and Dad, will you still love me? Will you keep me forever? How long do we have to keep the bald ones?

Doggies, please follow me. I'm about to lose it. Share and forward this post to your friends. Perhaps some of you have been through similar anxieties and can help calm my fears.

I'm too jumpy to sleep, but if the house ever quiets down again, I'll brave my way past Riley the recluse to give status updates on my miserable life.

MARCH 27

http://lexitriplets.blogspot.com

I wish I was a cat.

Are you there, followers? It's me, Lexi. Wow, 53 followers since my first post. Thank you for supporting me in my time of need. I feel the love.

I'm sorry I've been neglectful, but I'm exhausted--dog tired--no time to write these days. Things have gone from bad to worse.

Not only have I been invaded by the HAMs, but Grandma Strawberry (Mom's mom) and Gray Granny (Dad's mom) take turns staying here, nonstop. *Ugh!* Now, including the HAMs there are six of us, and often seven in my little castle.

The family room is overtaken by three rocking cradles. The babies are still too little to be alone in their cribs upstairs. So they sleep in the family room and are fed every three hours.

Tonight, Dad told Mom he'd take the midnight to 3:00 a.m. shift on the couch, so she could sleep in bed.

I snuggled with Mom upstairs. We'd been snoring softly when we were startled awake by the 3:00 a.m. alarm. Yawning and slurping the sleep from my eyes, I licked Mom's cheek to remind her it's time for the middle-of-the-night changing of the guard and diapers. After she wiped my slobber off her face, we staggered downstairs.

Midweek is Gray Granny's shift, since she's retired. So, my tail thumped on her door on my way through the hall. After all, if that woman is going to take up space here, she might as well get up and help.

Granny, with her gray hair askew, threw on her flannel robe and held the railing so she wouldn't trip on my squeaky toys lying on the stairs.

With only the light above the kitchen sink, Mom and Granny prepared bottles.

In the family room Dad struggled to sit up on the couch, yawned and felt around for his eyeglasses while his foot still rocked all three cradles.

I sunk into the loveseat next to him.

The babies with their eyes wide open squirmed while they made sounds like little lambs.

I stole this picture Mom posted on her Facebook page, captioning "Lexi's on duty for the 3:00 a.m. feeding." In reality, I was only in charge of diaper sniff patrol.

It's not fair. Hunter, Ava, and Max don't have to beg to be fed. In fact they don't even say a word, they just b-a-a- and bleat. I don't get fed every three hours. Nobody else does. I think they're spoiled. Maybe if the grownups fed them some real food, like my favorite, pepperoni and sausage pizza, the little ones might sleep longer and we'd all be happier.

The grownups moved without talking, their eyes only open a slit. Each picked up a baby who was trying to escape from the blankets wound like straight-jackets, only their faces sticking out.

Maybe if they were unwrapped, the HAMs would be happier because they could run and play like me. I could teach them to fetch and play Frisbee.

Mom, Dad, and Granny unwrapped the padding stuck with two strips of sticky tape around the little one's bottoms and cooed at them even though their nappies were full of poop.

I've always had to do my business outside in the sun, rain, or snow. The grownups take care of theirs in the big porcelain drinking bowl. No one tells us, "Oh, that's such a good poo poo. You must feel so much better!" when we have a code brown.

The other day, I did my *I-Can't-Hold-It-Any-Longer* dance until I leaked. I concluded no one would be mad because it must be all right to go inside--since the little ones do. Well, no one cooed or chuckled at me.

Gray Granny slid in the puddle and fell. It was her own darn fault. She wasn't watching where she was walking.

She turned over from her butt to her knees and stood up holding her hip, yelling "LEXI!"

Dad growled, "Bad dog, Lexi." He chased me outside, and left me there to shiver in the late-spring snow until he heard me scratching and whining. There was no treat for me when I came inside. I tried my usual trick of yipping to remind him, but Dad just shot me a glare.

If only they'd let me help, I could train the HAMs to doo-doo outside. I'm even willing to share my Pupperoni treats for rewards.

Well tonight, the feeding and diapering stole an entire hour of much-needed sleep. After everybody had a clean bottom, a full tummy, and was wrapped up again like a mummy, Mom plopped on the couch, Granny curled up on the love seat, and

Dad headed up to bed for another two hours until his alarm rings for work.

I nuzzled in with Mom, as she turned on the lullabies. I swear, if I hear "Rock-a-bye Baby" one more time, I'll puke.

I tried to extract myself from Mom's loosening, sleepy grip to sneak to the basement. Tiptoeing is hard for a dog because my toenails clack on the wood floor, so I'm careful to take steps only during the noisy inhale of Granny's snore.

The clock above the oven reads 4:15 a.m. as I escape to the cellar to fire up my computer.

I hoped I could creep by Riley without waking her. No luck. She glared at me from the rafters, her green eyes seething with envy. I muttered, "You have no idea of the craziness upstairs, Riley. You're lucky you can hide down here with no responsibilities for keeping this castle and its people safe. I don't know how much longer we can go on like this. The babies are already spoiled, and more work than they're worth."

Riley spit—*fffftt*—and arched her back so her hair stood on end. I scrambled to safety under my desk. Then she stretched, circled, curled up in a ball, returning to her luxurious slumber.

For the first time ever, I wish I was the carefree cat instead of the dutiful dog in this family.

Comment from Lucille the Labrador:

I hear you, Lexi. Sounds like you're in trouble and certainly need support.

Believe it or not, we actually have a growing network of tech savvy pooches sneaking to their owner's screens, when humans leave them unattended to make face-to-face conversations at the water coolers, or coffee pots, and especially during the hours they're crashed and sleeping.

Felines do not engage in our network, so your cat comments are safe here.

I relate to your jealousy about new humans. Baby Lucas arrived about 2 years ago. I was just beginning to understand that I'm Mom's protector and Lucas' playmate, then baby Lillian joined us and my job doubled.

Usually humans have offspring one at a time, not in a litter. I'm sure your three little humans will keep you trotting triple time, but you could consider yourself three times blessed to receive the HAMs all at once, Lexi.

In any case, know we're here for you. I will suggest all of my friends follow you so we can support each other.

APRIL 10

http://lexitriplets.blogspot.com

Mighty Max, Hunter Bear, and Piglet

Readers, thanks for sharing my plight. We've grown in numbers, up to 73 followers, due at least in part, to Lucille from last month, sharing my profile on her social medias.

I appreciate your comments. I especially love the picture Pookie the Poodle posted of her little girl tying pink bows in her curly ears. Bowser the Boxer posted a great tip on how to hold the hose on summer days to spray the babies.

You all give me hope that better days will

come, and someday these babies might be big enough to play with me. Can you advise; when will that happen?

Tonight, I'm sacrificing precious sleep to update my status. Hunter, Max, and Ava now weigh about as much as a small bag of dog food. I can tell them apart by the sounds they make.

Mom and Dad have nicknamed everyone in the litter. Just like they call me *Dressy Lexi* because I love my bling, *Pesky Lexi* when I'm in trouble, and *Lexapotamus* because I'm chubby, they call Maxwell *Mighty Max* just to make him feel big and strong, because he was the runt.

Every time they pick him up they coo, "Oh you're so mighty. You're such a Mighty Max." His cry is the most shrill. When he's not happy--and he is a grump much of the time--the entire house hears his soprano scream. You'd think someone was pinching him, but he's just hungry for those few sips of milk. His head is completely bald and he doesn't even have eyebrows or lashes yet.

Hunter's cry is a low baritone. Mom and Dad say it sounds like the neighbor kick-starting his motorcycle. When they pick him up they echo this sound back, kind of like they're having a conversation.

Gray Granny brought him a book about a little boy who wanted to grow up to be a hunter and pretended to search for a bear with a cap gun, so now everyone calls him *Hunter Bear*.

Sometimes when he's angry, Mom and Dad say, "Are you a *Grisly Bear*?" Other times when he's cuddly, they say, "Oh, you're such a *Teddy Bear*." Sometimes I hear them call him *Bear Cub*, or *Cubby* for short.

If you look closely you can see the fuzz of golden locks, and sprouts of blond eyelashes and brows--almost the same color as mine. His face is fatter than Max's because Max burns so many calories screaming.

Ava wants to eat all the time. She's getting round, pudgy cheeks that sag over her jaws. Mom and Dad call her *Piglet*. It's going to be embarrassing when she's on a softball team. She'll be mortified if Mom and Dad shout, "Go, Piglet!!" as she runs the bases.

Ava has the most hair, so Mom likes to spike that dark brown fluff into a Mohawk by lubing it with baby oil.

Ava's favorite sound is meowing. I roll my eyes because I think she does it just to annoy me. Sometimes they call her *Kitty Kat*. I guess it's a little better than Piglet.

All this growing, feeding and crying increases my workload tremendously, but worse is the fact that I have to take care of Gray Granny, too.

Since it's springtime, we've had thunderstorms. I hate thunderstorms. Long before the rain or thunder start, I hear a low buzz and my ears flatten against my head. My hair stands up between my shoulder blades as I shiver. My tail hides between my legs. Finally I get so nervous I start to pant.

In the past, whenever the weather scanner beeped, Mom or Dad would wrap me in this pretty pink striped thunder-shirt, cinching up the Velcro to make me feel secure and swaddled.

Then they'd let me cuddle with them on the couch, reassuring we'd all be safe.

But these days, they're swaddling babies and no one pays any attention to moi. No one even cares if we're in the path of destruction. What is wrong with these people!

Doggie friends, do you feel a storm before

it hits? I do. I think canines could do a better job predicting the weather than the meteorologists.

Yesterday the sun was shining, but I felt the storm coming. My ears started to buzz and I could feel an ache and tingling in my paws.

Mom and Granny were taking a quick break on the patio as the sun fought to spill through the growing clouds.

I sacrificed my own wellbeing to spring into action, trying to do the right thing, protecting the guest in the castle, gray-haired Granny. I slithered my head, then my front paws, and finally my rear onto her lap. Everyone laughed. How embarrassing.

But, I stayed on her lap, risking my own safety to protect her, receiving ridicule rather than gratitude.

The clouds thickened and raindrops the size of pennies plunked. Mom and Granny sauntered inside to turn on the TV. *Well, it's about time. Finally you're paying attention.* I whined as I heard the beeping and saw a dark blob on the radar passing over our end of town.

Through the night it rained cats and dogs. *Why do humans make up these sayings?* Granny slept on the loveseat, Mom on the couch, cuddling me while I trembled. The babies slumbered in their rocking cradles as the dim light over the kitchen sink flickered from the lightning.

I tried to doze, but a nightmare about the first time I met Gray Granny five years ago, flashed me back to puppyhood.

I'd been so excited I wound myself around her legs (I'd seen Riley

27

do this before) and I left a joy puddle on her pink shoe. Granny's hurtful words echoed through my dream. She asked Mom, "Can I borrow some dry socks?" and "Do you have a lint brush?"

Later that day, I'd tried to make peace by slinking next to her on the couch, pushing my cold, wet nose under her hand that held a partially eaten peanut butter cookie. I'd intended to lick her hand with kisses, but the remainder of her cookie accidentally dropped right in my mouth and I swallowed. I quickly slurped her hand, arm, the neck of her pink sweater, then pounced my paws on her shoulders to lick the cookie crumbs off her face.

But my cleansing, remorseful kisses were not good enough for her.

Granny bumped me off the couch to the floor. Then she went to the kitchen sink, and scrubbed her hands and face with soap and a paper towel.

So that's how it had started. That's how Granny and I got off on the wrong paw.

Shaken awake, brought back to reality by crashing and flashing, I was afraid we'd been struck.

Quick to forgive, springing into duty, my only motive was once again to protect the guest, whether she appreciated it or not.

Only feet away Gray Granny's snoring matched the roaring storm. I squirmed my body up on the loveseat, straddled hers, ready to lay down on top of her like armor, risking my life to save hers. Granted, she's almost as sleep deprived as the rest of us, but she woke up as spittle dropped off my panting tongue into her open mouth. Startled and screaming she woke the entire house. I jumped off the couch, rejected by Granny in my dreams and in reality. *It was an accident, Granny. I was just trying to help. You wouldn't scream like that if one of the babies spit up on you.* What an ingrate!

I scurried to the basement and the solace of my computer, and you—my friends. Things are not settling down around here. I'm trying my best to hold it together, but as warmer weather approaches, I'm getting a serious case of cabin fever.

I'm tired of being stuck in a house that smells like poo. I need fresh air.

I'm thankful to Winston, the Great Dane next door, for following my postings. He needs my help patrolling the neighborhood, chasing cats away from baby ducklings at the pond.

But, most of all, I feel replaced. Mom and Dad pay so much attention to the babies they'll never have time to play ball with me.

And, if Gray Granny never shows up again, it will be fine with me.

Comment from Tammy the Shih Tzu:

Lexi, I'm sorry to learn of your recurring nightmare about the rough start you had with Granny, but it does sound like she's redeeming herself and helping out now.

Maybe she's more trouble than she's worth, however.

She may come around, but maybe not.

Being as tiny as I am, usually people understand I'm a lapdog, but it seems unfair that you don't receive the same consideration.

I do believe your family has not rejected you because Mom shares the couch with you.

Yes, I too have a great fear of storms and

my doggie radar starts going off about an hour before the rain hits. Once it does, I'm hiding under, behind, or on anything or anyone who can offer me any comfort.

If the storm hits at night I shake so much that no one can sleep.

After all, I want my humans to wake up and comfort me, so I pant in their faces. I've been told my breath keeps them awake as well.

On a happy note, I love your triplet's names, and especially their nicknames. Bear, Mighty, and Kit Kat; Sounds like they could be characters in a great story.

APRIL 29

http://lexitriplets.blogspot.com

I love walks, I need walks, I want walks.

Outside the birds sing in the sunshine, perched in the sweet-smelling budding roses. Daffodils and pansies wag their heads. But, I'm stuck. Cooped up. Stir-crazy.

I understand taking the HAMs out is more work than it's worth, but don't they need some fresh air?

The only tolerable thing about Gray Granny is she loves walks.

But, Mom and Granny are careful not to say

the word "walk" around me because if my keen ears hear, I can't hold back my excited jitters which start with prancing and dancing in circles, emitting low, soft growls which intensify to happy yips, finally growing to sharp, high-pitched barks. So they've begun to use the code words "wash dishes" to mean taking a walk.

Mid-morning, after an hour and a half of feeding, burping and diapering, I heard these words floating through my naptime fog. Granny said, "It's a beautiful day. Do you think we could wash dishes?"

Well, I wasn't absolutely sure I'd heard correctly, and there certainly was a sink full of dishes, but the phrase just didn't make sense connected to the thought of it being a beautiful day. After all, I realize there are many chores to be done, but who in their right mind would rather stand at a sink full of dishes when it's a beautiful day?

So I rose from my nap posture, yoga-stretched my back (no wonder the pose is called downward dog) right down to shaking out the tips of my back toes.

I thought I've got to investigate, but play it cool.

Friends, you can't believe the production. All three babies screamed as Mom and Granny wrestled them into hats and coats. Not a centimeter of skin was exposed—except for tiny shaded faces.

Weren't Mom and Granny afraid the HAMs would melt? I imagined they'd dissolve, dripping with sweat.

By this time I was sure we were going for a walk because next Mom and Granny put on their walking shoes.

Then they helped each other buckle and snap Ava and Hunter into packs like book bags. But they didn't wear them on their backs; they put them on their chests. Max got the stroller.

I circle-paced in the hallway, trying so hard to be patient squelching my low growl as much as doggedly possible. I didn't want to be left behind.

Then Mom opened the front door and stepped out into the fresh air. Granny followed. They closed and locked the door. Locked me in. I freaked—completely lost my cool. Never so angry in my life, I cried, I howled. I jumped and clawed at the door. *You can't leave me in this prison. I'll fight my way out. I'm the one who should take walks, not those three pipsqueaks.*

I heard Mom and Granny step from the porch, then stop.

Mom said, "Uh-oh, Lexi's onto us. Maybe we should take her."

Granny, the evil woman, said, "Taking her along with three babies is just too hard."

Mom softened and said, "If you can push the stroller, I'll have an extra hand."

I love you, Mom. I love you, Mom. I love you, Mom. My tail wagged triple time.

I heard the key engage the lock. The door opened. Mom stepped inside and took my leash from the coat rack. Ava bawled while Mom bent down to hook the leash to my collar.

So excited, impossible to be still, I wriggled around Mom three times, tangling her in the leash. I think she wanted to scream.

All seventy pounds of me hopped like a spring bunny while we walked. It wasn't easy for Mom to hold my leash and keep Ava safe in the front pack, but she did it because I think she still loves me.

As we rounded the corner, I saw Winston, 110 pounds of Great Dane, sniffing and squirting next door while he played with his children, Taylor and Tyler.

I like Taylor and Tyler. They're good kids. Last school year, they waited at my house in the mornings for the school bus after their mom and dad went to work. They'd pass the time by playing tennis ball and sock tug-of-war with me. Their parents must have thought I was more responsible than Winston to look after the children. I'm certain it had nothing to do with the fact that my mom and dad were home because they went to work later in the morning.

Anyway, as we approached Winston's mom, watering her daffodils and tulips, we stopped to visit.

Winston's mom snapped this picture to document our first outing.

I introduced Winston to my triplets.

Did I say my triplets? Why would I do that? They're Mom and Dad's triplets, certainly not my responsibility.

Winston stepped forward to sniff Max, but I moved my body between them. *I'm not sure why, maybe because he's already got two kids, and I didn't want him to think he had dibs on my three.*

I don't want to offend my Great Dane followers, but you're just too slobbery to sniff tiny babies. You always leave shiny goober behind.

In the process, I sat on gray-haired Granny's toe. She scolded me, "Lexi, get back!" In her defense, I think she was afraid Winston and I would tip Max's stroller. *She doesn't get it. I was just trying to keep the kid from getting slimed.*

The ruckus ended Mom and Granny's conversation. As Mom pulled me away, Winston barked, "Message me through your blog, Lexi. Hang in there! Having kids in the house is not so bad. It's kind of fun when they play and snuggle."

I wonder about the snuggling part. I've never been in Winston's house. Does he leave his slobbery slime behind when he cuddles on the couch with Taylor and Tyler, and in their beds? Yuck.

I whined in reply, "Winston, I'll tell you more in my status update tonight. Thanks for your support. I hope to see you soon, if I ever get out of the house again."

For the remainder of our walk, I contemplated Winston playing fetch, chase, and hide-and-seek in the yard. Will my triplets have to grow to be Taylor and Tyler's ages before they can play with me? The HAMs are already three months old. When I was that age, Mom and Dad adopted me. I ate solid food. All I wanted to do was play. I'd jump. I'd run. I'd tug. I'd wear myself out playing. Then I'd fall asleep, wake up, and start the cycle again. Humans! They are just so slow!

Comment from Slobber-Mouth the Great Dane:

Lexi, I'm trying to understand and relate to your post, but I've never been on a walk. I run free because I'm so big. My humans aren't strong enough to control me on a leash.

They're pretty laid back so I'm loyal, staying in our yard or visiting close friends in the neighborhood.

Some love my gentle giant personality, others recoil because of my drool. It is not my choice to slobber, my breed has very loose lips and long jowls. When I drink water, the only way to dry my mouth is to shake my head and drool sometimes flies in people's faces or overhead. It ends up on everything; the windows, furniture, etc.

Please take it easy on your good neighbor, Winston. I'm sure he'd never hurt Hunter, Ava, or Max, although it might be good for your mom and Granny to carry some extra tissues or towels because our slime is inevitable.

MAY 10

http://lexitriplets.blogspot.com

Spring fever.

Mom takes pictures of us every week to post for friends and family. This week, since the roses are in full bloom, she wanted to pose us in the garden. She had an idea to put the HAMs in a wheelbarrow. First she moved both cars out of the garage and wrestled the wheelbarrow down from its hook on the garage wall. Then she lined it with soft blankets so she and Gray Granny could pose three squinting, squalling babies and snap quick pictures. The whole photo session took an hour to set up and tear down, but the babies were only outside for about two minutes.

Well, I'm swiping this picture to post for all of you. As you can see, I'm the only one smiling. The HAMs were dog-gone mad.

Afterward, Mom and Granny took the babies inside to feed and diaper. Then they put the babies in their cribs for a nap.

As soon as things calmed down, I heard Granny say to Mom, "Do you think L-E-X-I would like a W-A-L-K?"

Well, I certainly know how to spell my own

name and 'walk,' but I thought I'd better play this cool and not react for fear Granny might reconsider.

Gray Granny is a gritty woman—a tough old bird. She gardens, communes with nature, digs in the dirt and pulls weeds—a farm girl. She says, "Dogs should be treated like dogs."

Those poor fleabags at her house live outside, slaving away, protecting and herding the livestock.

Granny is not accustomed to walking pampered pooches like me.

I know she'd rather walk alone, but she probably thought about my last meltdown and was afraid my carrying on would wake the HAMs. She knew she'd get out of the house if she offered to take me, too.

Mom smiled and winked in response. Granny walked to the door to get her shoes. Trying to control myself, I sat down swishing my tail on the floor right in front of her, breathing hot breath in her face and slurping her forehead as she bent down to tie her laces. I raced her to the door with my feet slipping out from under me. She took my leash off the coat rack and tried to hook it to my collar as I danced in circles making a low moan--trying not to bark. *Don't wake the babies. Don't-wake-the-babies.*

I knew if the HAMs cried it would be all over. Granny and Mom would be back to rocking, feeding and diapering. This was my chance to escape and Granny was going to spring me out of this joint.

As soon as the door opened, I took off, nearly dragging her face first through the flowerbeds. Granny held on for dear life.

After she gained her footing, we wrestled for control of my leash. I fought to keep it long and slack so I could zig and zag from tree lawns to yards. She soon realized my leash was the retractable kind, and tightened it up. I was stuck at her side as if she'd super glued my ribs against her thigh. *I couldn't even sniff, and it was my favorite day to walk—trash day. So many smells. Yummy tidbits.*

Winston wandered in his yard. I wanted to disappear. I tried to be quiet and sneak by without being recognized, but just as we approached his sidewalk, Granny said, as if to settle down my pulling, "Good girl, Lexi. Aren't you glad to take a nice walk on a sunny day?"

Of course Winston raised his head to look. I was mortified, fearful he would laugh, or at least smirk. But Winston, my friend, sensed my agony and gave me one sad gaze, then quickly looked away so as not to embarrass me any further on my walk of shame.

I always enjoy one lap around the block, but that was not enough for Granny. She thought we both needed our exercise, so I was excited to walk two laps. Midway through the third lap my tummy started rumbling. Nature called. I was afraid this might drop out of me right in the middle of the sidewalk and some innocent child might step in the mush with new spring sneakers, or worse, bare feet.

Panicked, I twisted, writhed, and growled, fighting against that leash. Finally Granny had no choice but to give me some slack. I squatted and stooped inching my way toward the tree lawn. The soft mess plopped out, I circled around to sniff, making sure of my intestinal health. Then I sat waiting for Granny to reach down with the mini doggie trash bag and pick it up to carry it home for disposal.

But, Granny just looked at me.

On Granny's farm, dogs and all other kinds of animals do their business in the yard and it rots in the hot sun or is washed away by the rain. No one picks up dog poo in her neck of the woods. But here in the suburbs we must be polite to others who might follow in our path.

She and I stared each other down.

My unflinching glare conveyed, *Granny, I'm not moving until you pick that up. After all, you coo at the babies and smile when you clean their bottoms. You don't have to clean my backside, just pick up the remains!*

I even tapped my nose against the little blue plastic dog-bone shaped container of mini trash bags dangling from the leash.

Granny stared at me and rolled her eyes as if to say, "You've got to be kidding me, Lexi."

Well, finally she pulled out a bag and stuck her hand in it, then reached down to pick up the warm stinkiness. As she turned the bag inside out, a little brown smudge rubbed on the sleeve of her pink coat. She groaned, tied the bag, and said, "Ewww, yuck Lexi, couldn't you have held it till we got home?"

Still fixated on our fitness plan, as we rounded the house again, she dropped the bag off on our front porch and we began one final lap. I lagged.

I don't think I've ever done four laps. The old lady kept tromping, saying, "Come on, Lexi. You can make it."

Dusk crept in. The air cooled. Moms and Dads returned home from work. As we made the last turn, a silver-haired woman driving a silver truck approached, slowed, and rolled down her window. Granny smiled, probably because she and the woman had the same color hair.

The lady said, "What kind of a dog is that?"

Granny replied, "She's just a mutt." (Mom and Dad have always told me I'm a mutt, but they never used the phrase *just a mutt*. They tell me mutts are a combination of many kinds of dogs. That makes me feel like a queen. But Granny's words, *just a mutt,* made me feel sad.)

The silver woman continued, "She's gorgeous."

Wow! I lifted my head and held my tail high, glowing.

Then the woman stuck her head out of the window, looked me in the eye and said, "What's your name?"

Granny said, "This is Lexi. I'm just Lexi's Granny." When I heard Granny say she's *just* my Granny it made me feel like a star leading my personal assistant.

The woman said, "I hope to see you again soon, Lexi."

I strutted home.

Comment from Maggie the Mutt:

Lexi, I hate to break it to you, but mutt

is a term referring to a dog without a pedigree, of mixed parentage, not purebred. To the snooty, they look down their noses at us. To others, they think we are adorable in any size, shape or look. Some believe we mutts are less intelligent, but others believe we are smarter than most because we carry the best genes of all of our predecessors.

You are lucky your humans raised you with a strong sense of confidence, encouraging you to strut your Diva-self.

Lex, (may I call you Lex? I feel like we're good friends because I eagerly await all your posts), may I be so bold as to suggest you temper your responses to Gray Granny? She's an old farm lady and you're more the city girl. Simple misunderstandings can fester, if not healed. Sounds like she has a big heart to travel to help your family every week.

I know you feel like she comes to cuddle

the babies, and you probably wish she'd cuddle you, but in reality it takes two to make a friendship grow. In the meantime, she may be the only one to spring you out of the house from time to time.

JUNE 12

http://lexitriplets.blogspot.com

Overworked. Underpaid. Need more treats.

The HAMs are wearing tiny clothes now instead of swaddles and sleepers. In this week's picture Hunter, Ava, and Max are all dressed in their little monkey shirts and bibs. Do you see the monkey hat Mom bought for me?

Whenever Mom takes a picture, the HAMs are usually fussing. So, she calls me from important work, like guarding the front door or spying on the squirrels through the window. I drop what I'm doing and come running, toenails skidding on the hard floors.

All three little heads turn toward me as I bark to focus their attention.

I'm still a little unsure how close to wiggle in since my paws are about five times as big as the babies' hands.

Sometimes I sneak slurpy kisses on top of their heads. Mom and Dad smile, but Granny scowls.

My beard and whiskers are about two inches long, so I don't want to get too near for fear I'd let out a yelp if the babies pulled.

In this picture Granny put a Milkbone in Hunter's hand. Believe me, I wanted to eat it. My mouth watered. But I exercised self-control, leaving only a few drips of drool on the blanket before Granny finally let me eat the treat.

Hunter, Ava and Max were tired after this picture, so Mom and Granny put them down for a nap.

They've grown enough so they can sleep upstairs, although Mom and Dad still keep a rocking cradle close by for any crankypants.

Their small bedroom has three cribs. Since Dad's a techie, he's installed cameras over each crib so he and Mom can view the babies on their phones, tablets, and computers.

They should call me "Techie Lexi" because

they have no idea I hacked into the cribcam in Dad's security mainframe from last night to show that even though the rest of the house was snoozing, I was working like a dog at 2:00 a.m. guarding the HAMs in the dark of their room.

I regularly sacrifice my own sleep, until all three babies are sleeping, then I haul my weary body up on the end of Mom and Dad's bed and worm between for a couple of hours of shut eye.

Gray Granny sleeps in the spare room. She's an early bird. By 6:00 a.m. I slide down from Mom and Dad's bed to lie in front of Granny's door.

This morning her alarm buzzed at 6:15 a.m. She stepped over me to tiptoe to the bathroom. I heard the toilet flush, the water run, the hairspray spritz, and the buzz of Granny's electric toothbrush.

I paced in front of the door because I wanted my dental bone.

I have Mom and Dad trained to give me one each morning as soon as I come inside from my pottying. They call it my "coffee" because I'm grumpy until I get it. I only get one per day, so once I snatch it from their hand, I run to my soft doggie pillow by the fireplace and savor every morsel. *Let's go Granny, I need my dental bone as much as you need coffee!*

I was shaken back to reality when she opened the bathroom door and stepped over me again to return to the bedroom. She dressed, made the bed, swallowed her old-people medicine, and staggered out on the landing to head downstairs.

Now, don't get me wrong, I love to race, but I held back. It's still pretty dark when she gets up and she's usually carrying her phone, iPad, laptop, and baby laundry. The last thing I needed was for her to fall and break a hip in the half-light of dawn. Then I'd never get my dental bone.

We made our way downstairs to the back door. As I jumped on the door reminding her I had to go outside, she started to pull the door open. She tried to open, I jumped, shutting it by accident.

She opened, I shut.

She opened again, I shut again, until she said, "Please stop, Lexi!"

Finally, she got the door open and I bounded into mud puddles.

I tried to fake her out by looping around the rose bushes and coming back to scratch on the door. She knew I hadn't done my business, so she left me out in the drizzle.

I realized my bladder was full and I wasn't sure when anybody would have time to let me out again, so I slopped through the wet grass, mud squishing between my toes and stooped, then splashed back to the door.

I could see her through the fog of my breath on the storm door. She took her good ole' time putting baby laundry in the washing machine.

I pawed at the door a second, then a third time. She opened the door for me just as I heard a rumble of thunder. I shook to dry. She put her arms up to shield her face, as though I was pointing a hose at her, then tore paper towels, dropped them on the floor and swished them around with her foot as she scolded, "What a mess!"

Well, the cleanup was your own darn fault, Granny, for leaving me out.

Granny stalled by making her own coffee. It's called Fog Chaser. *Well, I need my fog chased too, Granny!*

I paced back and forth to the pantry where my beloved dental bones awaited.

The coffee machine dripped slow, brown caffeine.

She filled her cup, added cream, tasted, stirred, added more cream, and tasted again before I decided I'd had it!

I growled.

She glared.

I barked.

She shushed.

She turned to the sink, washed and sterilized a few bottles. I panted. I glared.

What about my coffee?

Did she forget my coffee?

I think she forgot.

I had to sneeze on her leg to remind her--
she always hates that.

Finally she moved to the pantry.

When Mom and Dad went to the grocery last
time, they bought generic dental bones since
they're pinching pennies with three more mouths
to feed. The new package held 15 bones, five of
them stuck together in a row, kind of like Kit
Kat candy bars, three rows in a package.

When Mom and Dad give me a treat, they
break off one small stick. But Granny, since her
fog was not quite lifted, took the entire block
of five treats out of the bag and began to move
her hand toward me.

Oh boy.

Oooh boy.

OH BOY, she's about to give me all five!

She hesitated, pulled her hand back, then
studied the picture on the front of the package.

Oh darn, she's breaking the clump apart. Deep sadness. She caught on.

She only handed me one, while she said, "Sorry Lexi."

I crept away to squeeze under the couch, cowering from the thunder with the solace of only one measly dental bone even though I deserved all five for what I have to put up with around here.

Within moments, I heard Max's soprano, Hunter's bass and Ava's meowing. Dad turned on the shower upstairs and Mom staggered down to the kitchen to start preparing the early morning bottles.

So, followers, that's the way my day started--tormented by the Ancient One and entrenched in monotonous routine.

Friends, I sincerely hope you relish every one of your pampered pooch days, because I can only escape back to mine through dreams after I collapse from the exhaustion of taking care of triplets.

A few months back life wasn't all about work.

I enjoyed my off-duty hours in the evenings cuddling on the couch and leading Mom and Dad around the block while decked out in my pink rhinestone collar.

Sometimes I'd even tug them to the neighborhood pond and show off by chasing the ducks.

Our little family of three was perfect; okay four, if you count Riley.

But those days are over.

Done.

Gone.

Now I multitask between babysitting and Granny training. I'll bet you know which of those is going better.

Comments from Punkin the Sheltie:

Lexi, Your babies, Hunter, Ava, and Max must be about four months old now. Things are becoming routine, even though there is so much growth happening just below the surface. The babies must be trying to roll over by now.

These things might seem small. We both know if these three were pups, they'd be running, romping, and playing with you by now. But, even these tiny steps in human development can be pretty exciting stuff.

Sounds like all of you are sleep deprived and cranky. Doldrums and monotony of feeding, diapering, and cleanup can get old.

But try to be patient. Listen for Hunter, Ava, and Max's giggles. Watch for their smiles. I know you can search for the joy and and find it.

My human and I have no little ones around

anymore. We live on a pretty large property and work very hard every day to keep up with Mother Nature. My human is a psychologist and writer, working mostly online so I've learned my computer skills from her. Every time she leaves the keyboard unoccupied, I sneak a peak at your blog, searching for new posts.

Because of her work in the behavioral sciences, I may have some tips to offer you. It's all about the attitude that exists between the ears. Positive or negative; life is what we make it, Lexi.

We all have our basic needs, like coffee, but I hope beyond that, Lexi, you can find the love in your life even though your family dynamic has changed, and it is not just you, and your mom and dad anymore. Now you have three more humans to love; Hunter, Ava, and Maxwell, and I hope you even come to like Granny.

Hard work, rather than a diva-lifestyle

creates happiness.

At the end of each day, my human and I tip back in the recliner in an exhausted peace, reflecting on tasks well done, even as our bodies ache. I hope you'll ease into that happy, satisfied exhaustion from knowing you've done good work for your family, too.

JULY 6

http://lexitriplets.blogspot.com

Vacuuming. Fireworks. Thunderstorms.

Dear Friends and Followers, I can't thank you enough for each and every "hang in there." Where would I be without you all?

With your encouragement resounding in my mind, let me get over myself and celebrate the good stuff.

Here's the HAM update:

Hunter smiles most of the time and loves to kick. He lies on his back and kicks so hard his whole backside lifts and scoots. I'm surprised he doesn't have bruises on his little heels from banging them on the hard floor. His motor scooter, kick-start cry has become more like an otter coughing, *aaarh, aaarh, aaarh.*

Mom and Dad are using *Kit Kat* for Ava's nickname now. Even though the name bristles my hide, I'm thankful they've given up on "Piglet." Not only does Ava make meow sounds, but now she can make a low, rumbling growl sound. I can't believe a sound like this can come out of a tiny human.

Max has a content little smile when Mom puts him in his baby swing. He turns his head to the right and snuggles his little nose up against the soft material while rocking back and forth to lullabies. Thank goodness we don't hear his soprano scream as often.

All three enjoy their mobiles but I'm their favorite entertainment. Every time I walk by they turn their little heads to gaze.

It gets even better. Every time I bark, they startle to attention. Mom, Dad, and Granny scold me if I let out a warning when the mailperson's truck slows. *Well, deal with it people. This is my job. Old habits are hard to break.*

Speaking of Gray Granny, she's still here three days a week. She comes on Tuesday morning and leaves before dark on Thursdays. I know Mom appreciates Granny and certainly needs her help, but I have to be honest and eek out a little complaint. The old woman gets in my way and spoils my naps.

Granny does dishes and laundry for Mom, but she vacuums *every day*. I hate the vacuum almost as much as thunderstorms. My hair is my crowning glory. Isn't that true of any girl? I've always been proud of the golden locks radiating from me like fairy dust or golden trinkets I sprinkle along my path.

Usually when Mom leaves to run errands, Granny pulls out the sweeper. The drone of the machine lulls the fussy babies as they sway in their swings, but it terrorizes me. I'm chased, hunted down, trapped. My paws get tangled in the cord.

Our castle is so small, there are few places to hide. After my throat becomes sore from growling when she gets too close to my toys, exhaustion overtakes me from jumping the sweeper cord, I zigzag-slink my escape, sneaking upstairs to burrow under the quilt on Mom and Dad's bed, trembling until the panic finally stops. Then I creep downstairs like a coward, nuzzling the HAMs necks or their bottoms, just to check to make sure they're unscathed.

Granny is not unfamiliar with dogs, so I don't think she absolutely hates me. During the years when Dad grew up, she and Papa had five different dogs ranging from an orphaned teacup poodle to a large German Shepherd. But she makes no secret that the dogs-in-her-house days are over as she empties the vacuum canister into the garage trash twice--once for upstairs and again for downstairs--saying, "Lexi, you're more work than three babies."

Well last Thursday Granny left a little early. She kissed Mom, hugged, cooed and gooed all over the babies, and gave me a quick pat on the head before she pulled on her pink shoes; the same pink shoes from our initial introduction. I can still smell the pee on them five years later, and because of that I felt a little guilty for the hassle I give her when she comes here to help us. I was going to give her a goodbye kiss to apologize but she was already out the door, climbing into her Jeep to head home for the weekend.

Soon after, Dad came home from work and helped Mom dress the babies for their first outing, an evening picnic.

I was a little skittish because I heard some popping outside. It sounded kind of like the beginning of a thunderstorm. Then I read the writing on the fronts of the boys' shirts, saying "My first 4th of July." Oh, no! I remember what July 4th is all about, *fireworks.* I am terrified by fireworks.

Mom put my red, white, and blue necktie around my neck and snapped a quick picture before they left. You can see I'm doing my job of barking and smiling, but that cheery look masks paranoia. Mom and Dad were too busy with the babies to even remember my thunder-shirt. All I could think about was where I'd hide.

I tried squeezing under the couch, but my backside wouldn't fit, leaving my tail vulnerable. Next I hid behind the recliner, but every time I bumped it just a little it rocked and pinched my tail.

I was desperate enough to seek out Riley for consolation, but the door to the basement was shut and I couldn't fit through the cat door. I only imagined Riley curled in a ball, purring, lulled to peaceful slumber by the rumble of the firecrackers, oblivious to my terror.

So, I ran upstairs thinking I'd hide under Mom and Dad's bed, or better yet, jump up on top and burrow deep within the covers. But, doggone it, Mom and Dad left the door closed, securely latched.

Next I thought I'd hide under Granny's bed, but three baby strollers were stashed there. The top of the bed was covered with laundry baskets full of sleepers, blankets and towels to be folded.

As last resort, I scurried into the bathtub in the bathroom Granny uses, shaking and hiding behind the shower curtain, as the pyrotechnics outside seemed to never end.

Really, I don't mind that Mom and Dad wanted to go to a Fourth of July picnic to show off the HAMs. *But, where the heck was Granny when I needed her?*

Due to my stress level, I must have curled up and escaped into sleep, because hours later I startled awake as I heard the door open. I thought, *Come on now, Lexi, pull yourself together,* as I jumped from the tub and tried my darndest to casually saunter downstairs while bravely holding my head high, even though when

Mom and Dad petted me they could feel my still racing heartbeat.

The pop-popping didn't stop until the wee hours, and I couldn't control my shaking until I was nuzzled between them in bed.

The holiday weekend seemed to boom and pop for days.

To top it off, yesterday we had a thunderstorm and the tornado siren blared, so we all headed to the basement, Ava in Mom's arms, Max in Dad's and Hunter in a bouncer Dad hauled downstairs. Mom spotted my thunder-shirt on a shelf amongst outgrown and yet-to-grow-into clothes for the babies. Dad helped me into it. Despite their efforts, I paced and panted, and I'm still wearing it as I finish this post to you, my friends.

I kept my secret about the bathtub-hiding place until this morning when Granny arrived and asked Mom if she had any idea why there were paw prints in her shower.

I hope Dad doesn't look through security footage, or he'll find this picture.

Comment from Shelia the Irish Setter:

Lexi, I'm nervous by nature, so the entire triple whammy you mention, the vacuum, fireworks, and thunderstorms, create terror in me as well.

I admire you because before you even wrote about the trauma, you took time to count the triple blessing of Hunter, Ava and Max.

I've heard humans say, "All's well that ends well," and your situation ended well. Your family took you to safety with them and even wrapped you in your thundershirt.

You're even making progress with Granny, by admitting she'd have been better than nothing.

Keep working on her, Lexi. She'll come around.

Thanks for teaching me the important lessons about seeking the positive, even in the negatives, and remaining calm.

AUGUST 10

http://lexitriplets.blogspot.com

Grandma and Granny; Good and Evil

I apologize ahead of time, I know I shouldn't be saying nasty things, but I *have* to vent.

If I could choose between the two old women, I'd choose Mom's mother, Grandma Strawberry. She works as a nurse, so she spends weekends with us. She arrives on Friday nights, coming straight from the hospital, still wearing her scrubs with her wavy red hair pulled up in a ponytail. Maybe the red hair explains why she has a passion for strawberries. Not only are they her favorite food, but she collects everything to do with strawberries. She must have a hundred pictures and knickknacks of strawberries in her house. Every time she visits, she brings strawberry clothing for Ava. I recognize her ring tone, "Strawberry Fields Forever" as she calls Mom to tell her she's almost here.

Even though Grandma Strawberry's pets were cats while Mom was growing up, I've convinced her that dogs are better because I smother her with kisses when she arrives, snuggle with her on the couch, and she even lets me crawl on the end of the bed sometimes. (Shhhh, don't tell Gray Granny a mongrel has been on the bed!) In return, Grandma Strawberry brings the HAMs and me presents every time she visits.

Last weekend I was wild with excitement because she brought me strawberry doggie biscotti from a real doggy bakery. The white bag was sealed with a lovely gold sticker shaped like a doggie, adding a distinctive touch of class.

Every time I marched out for a potty break and returned, Grandma Strawberry gave me an entire biscotti. She didn't even break it in half.

On Tuesday morning Gray Granny was back. Instead of presents she brought new underwear called onesies for the HAMs. *What kind of a woman brings her grandchildren underwear? Wouldn't they rather have toys?*

I thought, I'll make the best of it, so I greeted her at the door with my bottom-wiggling, happy dance. She said, "I'm sorry Lexi, I didn't bring anything for you. I'll bring you something next time."

A few hours later after the morning's vacuum terror was over and the babies were napping, Granny browsed through snacks left on the kitchen counter from the weekend. She opened my strawberry biscotti bag, pulled one out, sniffed, and took a bite. She coughed, and *pitoooey,* a bite of my luscious biscotti was spit in the trash.

As if that wasn't bad enough, before I could jump to grab the remainder of the bag from the counter and run to hide, Granny mumbled, "Yuck, this is stale," scooped up the entire bag and tossed it in the trash. I slunk away, hid behind the couch sniffing back my tears.

That evening, Dad pulled the garbage to the

curb for pickup the following day. Dad sealed up the bag and set it at the curb. In the twilight, I gazed at the bag out the window, longing for my special treat. Then I saw Winston ambling down the sidewalk, lifting his leg on trashbags on his way up and down the street. He stopped, sniffed, and pawed a hole in ours. I saw the glint of the golden doggie sticker as he pulled out my white bakery bag and carried my biscotti home to his yard. He didn't even glance my way or yip a thank-you.

Oh well, I guess I'd rather have a friend enjoy the delicious treat than have it decay in a landfill. It's true what they say, "One dog's trash is another dog's treasure."

One saving grace about having Gray Granny in the house is that she likes to bake. This week she made luscious, gooey cinnamony apple pie and rich, moist pumpkin bread. As she and Mom snacked, I worked diligently to impress with my crumb cleanup. They rewarded me with the last, mouth-watering bite.

Well, after Granny left this evening, and before Dad came home, Mom struggled to feed all three fussy babies. As she rushed to the kitchen to clean up bottles, she heated the last piece of pumpkin bread in the microwave. A thick slab of butter melted on top. I could see the steam and smell the pumpkin spice as that piece lay waiting to be eaten on a pretty orange paper plate at the edge of the end table.

Now, you'll remember that feeding requires diapering: *gotta get rid of what comes out before new stuff goes in.*

While Mom's back was turned to change Ava's diaper, I just swiped my tongue beside the plate on the end table, thinking perhaps I might clean up a stray crumb. My tongue edged too close, causing the plate to drop to the floor and the whole piece of pumpkin bread found its way between my teeth. Mom heard my scuffle and turned. She ran to the baby rocker, laid Ava down and chased me, yelling, "Bad dog, Lexi!"

It gets worse. She caught me by the tail and pushed her fingers in my mouth to swipe out every bit of that bread. Well, if she didn't want me to have it, at least she could've eaten it, but *No*, she threw that piece of scrumptiousness directly in the TRASH and shrieked, "Shame on you, Lexi!"

What? Neither of us get to eat it?

With my tail between my legs, trying hard not to leak, I slunk upstairs to the quiet emptiness of Granny's room.

Mom didn't call after me to apologize. Still, I tried to forgive.

Soon Dad arrived home. I heard him kiss Mom and goo-goo at the babies.

Earlier in the day, Mom put a pot roast in the oven. I could smell the deliciousness even upstairs. Scooting down to the floor from Granny's bed, I crept to the top of the stairs, and heard Mom tell Dad about the pumpkin bread. They chuckled.

I thought maybe Mom had forgiven me and I'd better get back to my duties of crumb cleaning, so I rushed downstairs. Mom and Dad ate dinner *yumming, oohing, and aahing,* as though it was the best meal of their lives, but the worst part? They didn't even give me a single scrap from their plates.

I was stuck eating dry kibble.

Lesson learned. Haste makes waste. If I hadn't been in such a hurry to eat that whole piece of pumpkin bread, Mom would have shared it with me, and I would have gotten some pot roast for supper, too.

So, as you can see, friends, it's been a

rough time here. The next time I see Winston, if I ever get out of this house again, I'm going to ask him if he could help me escape. Maybe he'd leave his basement window open and I could sneak in. I think he'd bring me bits and pieces of food now and then. He'd share enough to help me survive, and the vet does say *I need to cut back on scraps and watch my weight.*

It would sure be hard leaving the babies now, because they are getting kind of cute. But maybe, when they get older and can finally play outside in the yard, I could sneak peeks at them and Mom and Dad through the basement windows.

I'm so sorry, Mom. I promise I'll try not to steal food again.

When Mom wasn't looking I sneaked her phone and snapped this selfie. I'm practicing my "I'm sorry" face.

Comments from Winston, your neighbor:

Hey Lexi, that biscotti was fantastic! I thought maybe you had your fill since you're more of a delicate eater. I'm basically a scrap scavenger and will eat any rank leftover found anywhere, so I was thrilled to consume the remainder. Sorry for the misunderstanding.

I'm doubly sorry that you did not get to enjoy your Granny's pumpkin bread.

I do smell some pretty good aromas of fresh baked goods wafting from your house when she's around.

I'd advise making the best of it. Please don't run away.

Of course I'd help you if you ran away to my house, but if I hid you in my basement, you'd never get outside and you'd have to survive on left overs from my junk-yard dog diet. I scavenge pretty hard for those and don't have a lot to spare.

I'm pretty sure you'll be forgiven. The "I'm sorry" face will touch your mom's heart. We all need to practice that face to keep on reserve for tough times.

SEPTEMBER 15

http://lexitriplets.blogspot.com

Cramped. Overcrowded. A dog needs to breathe.

Hunter, Ava, and Max are almost able to sit up by themselves now. During some waking hours, Mom puts them in three contraptions called bouncers. Hunter jumps and stomps so hard on the floor that Mom and Dad call him *the noisemaker*.

Combined with playpens, changing tables, three baby swings, strollers, and toys, our little castle is overcrowded. Sometimes when I walk through the narrow pathways between babies, furniture, and equipment, Ava tries to pull my tail. She'll yank out a handful of my fur and then try to stuff it in her mouth. Gray Granny thinks that's disgusting.

I agree.

She's finally right about something.

See what I mean about the clutter?

Often, after the babies are in bed, I overhear Mom and Dad talking about the house being too small. They don't think the two boys and Ava can sleep in the same room forever.

Well, if we stayed right here, and Ava needed her own girly room, she could boot Granny out and redecorate. But, I can't talk; no one would listen to me anyway.

Mom, Dad, and I spend our evenings watching home improvement TV shows like *Fixer Upper*. Dad thinks we should build a room in the basement. *Yuck, cat litter is all I can say!* Besides, if we did that, we'd be left with even less room for storage, a small garage, and a house that sits dangerously close to a busy street.

My favorite show is *House Hunters*. I don't want to miss a moment because the featured family is usually comparing three homes to see which one will work best for their needs. There is so much for me to learn and I get mad at Dad when he switches to news or sports if Mom leaves the room.

Mom believes we should move into a larger house with a larger yard. We don't need fancy and new. Mom and Dad are hard workers and don't mind using elbow grease to improve an older home. Dad's pretty good with electrical and plumbing projects and Mom is great at decorating.

I'm sure Gray Granny and Grandma Strawberry could help me with the babysitting.

I've watched Mom search Realtor.com and send Dad links to houses that might work for us in our area.

I've been so busy that I've had difficulty finding time to update my blog lately because I continue the search for houses into the wee hours from my basement office, long after everyone else has collapsed in bed.

But, may I ask you, Cyberfriends, what would be on your wish lists for good houses for dogs and babies?

The overcrowding is nearly unbearable especially now that it's September, and that means football season! Everybody in this house is a big Ohio State fan.

On Saturdays all work stops and the front door is flung open for family and neighbors to come in, hang out, and cheer for the Buckeyes.

Oh, the food, bratwurst, pizza, chili, you name it!

Winston and his family come through the back gate, his mom carrying her famous taco dip. While she's inside watching the game, Winston teaches me to play football with Taylor and Tyler. I think it will be forever until Max, Hunter, and Ava can pass, catch, and score touchdowns.

The HAMs are still too little to pay attention to the game but Mom bought them Ohio State shirts anyway. Since Max's nickname is Mighty, she found one for him that read, "I'm a Mighty Ohio State fan since birth!"

Even though I love posing for family photos in any costume from Cupid to Santa, Mom and Dad forgot about me, but I remembered my scarlet and gray shirt that reads "poop on Michigan" and raced to the basement to tug it out of a pile of my old outfits.

I carried it upstairs in my teeth and laid it in the middle of the standing-room-only crowd as everyone watched Ohio State vs. Michigan. Even though I've gained a few pounds from all the football game goodies, I carry my full figure well. So, Mom and Dad squeezed me into my shirt—then snapped a picture of all four of their children.

Do you see Ava's bow? I wish I had one too.

Oh my gosh, it's already 1:00 a.m. So, as I close for tonight, with a belly full of football party cleanup, think of me and wish me luck with the search for our new house.

I anxiously await your suggestions and wish lists. Maybe there's a great house for sale in your neighborhood and we could extend our friendship from the online kind to those of real neighbors.

Comments from Darlene the Doberman:

Hi Lexi! I love your blog, never miss a post, and now I feel I have something to add.

We pets adapt well and will do anything to make our humans happy, but let's face it, the humans make the decisions for us and often we are squeezed in as an after thought. I certainly understand the overcrowding issue.

My life started out with Dave, when he graduated from college. I wandered, lost at the side of the road, when I was too young to have a well-developed sense of direction. He scooped me up and put me in his truck and we've been together ever since. He saved my life and in turn, I'd sacrifice my own to save his.

In the years since Dave took me in, he met Allison and they married. Allison loved me as much as Dave does. We were a very happy threesome.

Now, two toddlers later, we are cramped in a two-bedroom condo because Dave has just been transferred for his work, again.

We live in Chicago and either Dave or Allison has to take me down the elevator to the park across the street to relieve myself. We are so cramped I feel like a bull in a china shop whenever I turn around.

I hear Dave and Allison talk about their wishlist, a yard and a sense of community.

Dave grew up on a farm, so he'd like acreage, a barn and animals. Allison is not so sure she wants to be a farmer's wife, but she'd like a park to play in for the kids and good schools.

Dave is handy, so he'd like a place he can tear apart and put back together.

Allison has her doubts about Dave putting a house back together.

The important things my family wants, you already have, Lexi, so count your blessings. It all comes down to sorting out needs from wants. We need love. You and I already have that from our humans. Whether we get the things we want or not, we know love trumps things any day.

OCTOBER 31

http://lexitriplets.blogspot.com

Diarrhea, De-worming, Dress-ups

A couple of weeks ago Mom noticed my tummy was making loud noises. I think this affliction happened because I've been drinking out of puddles in the yard.

That same day Granny detected a slimy brown spot on the floor, wiped it up, suspected it wasn't melted chocolate, then put it close to her nose for the sniff test. "Ewwww, I think this came from Lexi."

Mom replied, "Just what I need, one more

butt to wipe." So she began to clean me with baby wipes every time I came in the house.

Humiliating.

Well, as if Mom doesn't have enough to do, she made me an appointment with the veterinarian who prescribed magic de-worming medicine.

Things have been so busy at our house that I'd missed my regular appointment, so the doctor did a complete examination of my other parts, too. As he looked in my mouth, he told Mom my teeth need to be brushed regularly. Now, Mom is a calm, pleasant person. She never disagrees, but she did ask the doctor, "How am I supposed to do that with triplets at home?"

The doctor replied, "I think Lexi might like having her teeth brushed because I have peanut butter flavored toothpaste."

I slunk out of the office with Mom following behind carrying the de-worming medicine, a doggy toothbrush plus a tube of toothpaste.

At home, Mom tried to hide my pills in salami. But I thought I'd trick her by eating the chunk of salami and spitting out the pill. Quickly, I reconsidered, because I really need this tummy ache to go away. Honestly, I didn't even taste the pill; it slid down as I scarfed the salami.

Then she gave me some toothpaste to lick. It tasted like gritty peanut butter, not my creamy Jiffy. I kept licking my tongue against my teeth to try to get it out of my mouth.

My beard is one of my cutest assets, but while Mom was wrestling me trying to get the toothbrush to my back teeth, she had to grab my beard to hold my mouth open. After I finally wriggled away I ran upstairs to hide in Granny's room, hoping Mom would be too busy to find me.

The next afternoon, as Mom was getting ready to run some errands, I overheard great news. Grandma Strawberry was coming early! She actually arrived while Mom was out.

The doorbell rang and Gray Granny answered while holding Ava to her shoulder. I jumped, yipped and twirled around hoping Grandma Strawberry would hug me, pet me, love me and hand over a bakery bag of biscotti. Instead she rushed to the family room and picked up Hunter. She and Granny proceeded to have a goo-goo fest, their lips puckered in kiss-like pouts saying things like "Oh, you're just such cutie pies! I love you all so much!"

Grandma Strawberry said, "Wasn't it nice of my daughter and your son to have enough babies that we each get to hold one? There is even one left over for Lexi."

They didn't see me roll my eyes, but they heard my nails tapping on the floor and glanced at me, realizing I was doing my I-have-to-potty-now dance. As Granny put Ava down so she could let me out the backdoor, I heard her explain my intestinal condition to Grandma.

Granny kept a close eye on me through the window, so I wouldn't drink out of any puddles. Then she let me back inside. Gray Granny and Grandma Strawberry both saw something dangling from my bottom, and Grandma Strawberry quickly said to Gray Granny, "Well, I'm holding a baby. You'll have to do the honors."

As if having Mom wipe my backside hadn't been bad enough, having Granny do it was *mortifying*.

I tried to keep my tail tucked between my legs, but that just made matters worse. Stink stuck to my entire backside.

Gray Granny pulled up my tail and scrubbed, while wrinkling her nose and holding her breath. Wouldn't you know it, she was wearing that same pink sweater—her favorite—the one from our first introduction, the one I saw in my nightmare. Not wanting to soil it again, I finally collapsed on the floor and rolled over in surrender as though I was one of the HAMs being diapered.

After she'd gone through more than a handful of wipes, she let me go and ran to the sink to wash her hands three times, then followed up with a generous squirt of sanitizer.

I ran, jumped, and curled up tight to Grandma Strawberry on the couch. *Protect me Grandma Strawberry, please.*

Since Grandma was now on duty, Gray Granny knew she could pack to leave. As she lugged her suitcase down the stairs, I overheard her say, "Oh no, Lexi's teeth haven't been brushed."

I trembled. In one movement I slithered off the couch and tried to wedge myself underneath. I got caught at the shoulders. I kept poking my nose further toward the wall so at least my mouth was hidden from her. But, no, Granny was determined to win this round.

She sat on the floor, pulled my pink collar, hauling me out and started trying to entice me with the peanut butter toothpaste.

Yuck.

I didn't want that grit in my mouth, but she pulled my beard down and swished my lips back with the heel of her other hand, while she went after my entire mouth.

I finally gave up the fight because I didn't want to hurt her in our tussle. You know, the woman has bad knees. But as soon as she was done, I wedged my head under that couch and didn't come out again until I heard the door close behind her. Only then did I emerge and snuggle again on the couch next to Grandma Strawberry.

I just can't leave this out because now, after a few days, my tummy is better and my teeth cleaner, and I'm very excited because tonight is

Halloween.

Mom worked in the fashion industry for many years before having the triplets and took great pride in dressing Riley for every holiday, especially Trick or Treat since she's Halloween black. But this year Mom bought costumes for the babies and me, too! The babies were dressed up as monkeys, and I was the banana. No mention was made of dress-ups for Riley.

Dad had planned to be home because he and Mom wanted to show all of us off around the neighborhood, but he had to stay late at work.

But, friends, my Mom is not to be deterred. She laid a soft, fuzzy blanket in the doorway and put me in charge of all three babies while she passed out candy to little princesses, super heroes, and monsters.

It was a glorious night, but I'm a bit troubled wondering if I'll be reduced to Riley's level with no costume at all next year.

Here in the wee hours, I'm enjoying seeing the photos you've posted of your Halloween costumes. But dear Winston, I'm so sorry Taylor and Tyler posted this humiliating picture of you on their Facebook page. A dog wearing cat ears; could it get any worse?

Comment from Deeno the Dachshund:

Hi Lexi. I love the Halloween pictures! How creative of your mom to dress you as the banana for your three little monkeys.

My costume lacked even an iota of creativity. Can you believe my mom dressed me as a wiener? The Weiner Dog joke for a Dachshund is tired and old. I would rather have had no costume.

But I have to cut my family some slack. We also have little humans running around, age two, three, and four. Mom and Dad are both working and frazzled. Actually, I was lucky to receive a Halloween costume at all.

We don't live near family, so I am envious of your stories about your life with visiting grandmas, even if they sometimes get too personal. Even though your house is overcrowded with babies and visiting family, it's better than being lonely and missing them.

Poor Winston. I agree, wearing kitty ears for a dog of any kind, let alone a large breed, is akin to public shaming.

Be careful and don't drink out of any more puddles. Nothing's worse than that kind of bellyache.

NOVEMBER 18

http://lexitriplets.blogspot.com

Nose to the ground. House hunting. Hounding new digs.

Friends and followers, thank you for all your wish-list comments about features that would make a house a home for kids and their doggy. Behind the scenes, for two months, I have been tirelessly searching real estate websites looking for the perfect property.

Mom and Dad continue their search, too. Granny stays with babies while they visit houses, but I overhear them talking about small, postage-stamp-sized yards, busy streets, too much traffic, too far from work, high crime area, not enough bedrooms, garages not big enough for toys, and most of all too much money.

But, here is the reality of our overcrowding. I'm writing to you from the dungeon of the basement in which I can't begin to find Riley among all the paraphernalia. We have enough toilet paper, paper towels, diapers and baby wipes to supply us for months.

Even though the babies are only eight months old, there are items stacked here and there that they've already outgrown, such as newborn clothing and baby blankets as well as items they will grow into like riding and push toys.

Mom and Dad like to stockpile canned goods down here since we don't have a pantry upstairs. So in addition to what Mom, Dad, and I eat, the shelves overflow with baby food.

Baby bottles have taken over the kitchen.

There never was room for a kitchen table and there certainly isn't room for three highchairs, so Mom and Dad plunk all three babies into the triplet table.

Eating? Yes, the HAMs are eating food now. It looks like slime. The stuff is brownish, greenish, yellowish sludge in small jars. The baby's gums are just beginning to sprout tiny white teeth, but they certainly can't chew anything, so this sludge just slides down through their mouths to their tummies. Correction--about half of it ends up on their faces, clothes, and the floor, until I hear Mom call, "Lexi, clean up in aisle Ava."

If I leave any morsel, she taps her toe and says, "Lexi, you missed a spot."

Ava Girl's favorite food is prunes. The tip of Hunter Bear's nose has an orang-ish tinge from eating so much squash. Mighty Max blows bubbles through carrots and sweet potatoes.

Honestly, the stuff doesn't taste half bad. Mom and Granny put the empty jars on the kitchen floor for me to lick before they are put in the recycling.

Mom tries to save money by making some of their food. With all the bottles and formula stacked about, she has about one square foot of counter space for the blender and baby food containers.

My dog dish has been moved by the backdoor, and at times I've thought it might end up in the backyard. Mom and Dad have nowhere to eat except the TV room, and that space is overloaded with playpens, bouncing toys, three swings and every kind of baby equipment times three.

The babies roll now, so I stand guard and make sure they're not getting in harm's way. A few days ago at a moment when my eyelids drooped with sleep, I jolted awake to see Granny extracting Hunter from under the couch. Yesterday I ran to the door to bark for the UPS person and I returned to find Max sucking on one of my rawhide bones under the TV table.

The floor is made of dark brown vinyl, which keeps my hair rolling in dust bunnies all over the place, but Mom and Dad are concerned that when the babies start to stand and walk, the hard floor will be dangerous if they fall.

To give them a soft landing pad, Mom bought a big, spongy ABC puzzle mat at a garage sale that takes up almost the entire room. There is barely enough space for the adults to step over and around it, but it's very hard for me to jump over. Sometimes I forget and sit on the mat. Mom yells, "Lexi, get your butt off!" She doesn't want my bottom to be where the babies are drooling.

Upstairs, Mom and Dad's room is overflowing with a playpen, a swing and a cradle, too, just in case the HAMs are fussy in the night. The triplet room is bulging with three cribs, monitors, a humidifier, a dresser, and changing table.

Before bedtime tonight we all squeeze into the bathroom overflowing with an inflatable baby bathtub and squeaky toys. Mom begins the assembly line of bathing each baby, then hands that one off to Dad who trots to the nursery to diaper and dress each for bed. This process is repeated three times for three babies.

The whole ordeal seems such a waste of time. If they were my pups, I'd just lick them clean. Even as a grown dog, I'm fine with a bath maybe once a month. But Mom and Dad wash them with stuff that makes me sneeze. Then they rub them with lotions and ointments, making them sticky all over again. At least all of this washing makes the HAMs smell better than the stuff I sniff in their diapers.

Mom and Dad deflate the baby bath time equipment and stow the toys in buckets, knowing it will have to be moved out of the bathroom to the hallway tomorrow morning if either of them can steal time for a shower.

When we put the babies to bed, there is no way all three can fit on one lap for a bedtime story, so Mom and Dad lay them all in one crib, saying, "Party in Hunter's crib!"

Tonight I overheard Dad tell the triplets

he was reading the same book to them Gray Granny read to him when he was a baby.

To add to our claustrophobia, the weather is chilly and gloomy. Freezing rain will soon give way to snow. Granny says her bones hurt, and it's too cold for walks. We have cabin fever and winter hasn't even really started.

Thanks for sticking with me as I moan.

Comment:

Hi Lexi, This is Marley, the Labradoodle across town. The big, vacant house across the creek from me has been for sale for a few months. It needs work, but has a big yard, woods in the back and is on a quiet street located about 30 minutes from you.

Maybe you can forward the link to your mom and dad.

Would be cool if we could be neighbors.

DECEMBER 26

http://lexitriplets.blogspot.com

We're buying a house!

Not to brag, friends, but we're buying *MY* house!

Can you tell that I'm wiggle-butt excited! *Can't wait. Can't wait. Can't wait!*

But, let me back pedal to fill you in on details.

Shortly after Marley's comment, I anonymously sent the link to Mom and Dad's email, and they went to take a look. When they got home I heard them say things like, "dirty carpets, neon green bathroom, fuchsia colored bedrooms, needs work."

But they also said things like, "laundry room, pantry, front room could be a playroom," and most importantly, "the price is right."

So they took the plunge and bought *my* house while selling this one all in a month.

With Hunter, Ava, and Max just nine months old, trying to sit up, rolling everywhere, eating nonstop, barely sleeping, this was not an easy task.

Taking the babies anywhere is tough, but going to the new house to work has been almost impossible.

Every morning, Mom and Granny dressed the babies in their warm fleecy sleepers, then they collapsed and folded up the mini baby beds called pack and plays and loaded them in the car along with baby bouncers, two carpet cleaners, and painting supplies and headed to the new house.

I have no idea what happened while they were there because I only saw them drag back home with carry out bags from McDonald's, late at night, too exhausted to speak.

With everyone being gone out of the house for such long hours, I have to admit, my mind went back to the panic I felt before Mom and Dad brought home Hunter, Ava and Max. It's taken me months to settle into this new normal. I fretted, were we beginning another transition that could be as difficult?

In addition to working on the new house, it was beyond difficult to sell a house that was bursting at the seams with triplets and mountains of their equipment.

On the night before the realtor came to take pictures of our little castle, there was an unbelievable flurry of activity after the triplets went to bed. Mom, Dad, and Granny removed every bit of baby stuff from inside the house, stashing and stacking it in the garage and basement.

The next morning Mom shooed Dad, Granny, and the babies out of the house a mere ten minutes before the realtor's photographer arrived. As Dad and Granny were hoisting the babies into car seats to go to work at the new house, Mom was meticulously ironing the dishtowel to hang over the stove handle.

There was no room in the car for me, so I knew I had to do my best job to help Mom. She always wants me to step into pictures and requests that I bark. I assumed this was my job. This must be why I'd been left behind. But the realtor found me annoying, stepped on me, tripped and nearly fell. I was banished to the basement with Riley.

After the photo session, what already was a crowded house became a dark maze of empty cardboard boxes and bubble wrap waiting for packing.

I paced, I worried, I wrung my paws, thinking *What have I gotten my family into? What can I do to help?*

I wish I could have had a conversation with Mom and Dad, but instead I sent Mom an anonymous email saying, "Why don't you leave the triplets at home with your responsible dog, Lexi? She could help you by babysitting while you're in the midst of your move. In an emergency, she could call Winston."

Mom read it while groggy-eyed, deleted it quickly, glanced at me and mumbled, "Lexi? Noooo. Must be spam. Hope I haven't been hacked."

I was left behind for weeks as more and more stuff was moved out of the old castle and taken to the new.

I started to panic. Paranoia set in. I wondered, *Will they take me? Or will I be left behind?*

I'd overheard Granny talking with Mom saying, "Are you sure you want to take Riley to the new house? Maybe she'd be better off going to the farm."

Mom would tip her head and shrug her shoulders as if she was contemplating.

Well, I know about farms. I've heard Granny's stories--cows, pigs, sheep, open fields. Farms sound like fun places. It could be a nice home for Riley being out in nature instead of cooped up in the basement. Who knows though, perhaps her allergies would get the best of her.

But lurking in the back of my mind was the way Granny said the word *farm*--almost in a whisper, kind of like it was a code word for something ominous.

Then I got nervous, wondering if Mom and Dad would take me to the farm, too. After all the work I'd done to find a new castle, would I be able to go?

In addition to all that was happening, Christmas quickly approached. Mom and Dad drove an hour to Grandma Strawberry's house for Christmas Eve. It was a short trip so they didn't have to spend the night. But the trip to Gray Granny's house required an overnight stay because Granny and Papa live two and one half hours away.

Granny left here three days ago in the lead vehicle, to prepare for our visit. She had the choice to pack the car full of baby stuff, like three pack and plays, clothes, bottles, formula, sterilizers, diapers, baby food, and toys; or she could have taken me on the road trip to her house. There was not room for me along with all the stuff plus the three babies in Mom and Dad's car. Guess what she chose? She chose the stuff. In fact, she even suggested I stay in the doggie hotel instead of coming to her house for Christmas at all.

I was sad that I didn't get to go on the road trip and spend a couple of extra days with Granny and Papa. She makes this drive all by herself every week. I would have been her wing-dog, protecting her the whole way.

I'm afraid that I didn't leave a good impression last year when I was so excited to see the entire family for Christmas and I used her green living room carpet as though it was grass outside. She bought a carpet cleaner after that visit.

Well, yesterday we all made it to Granny and Papa's for this year's Christmas.

Dad's sister and her husband were there

too, with their little girls, Lizzy and Abby.

They don't have a dog, but they want one so badly that they chase me around until I'm breathless and have to collapse behind the lazy boy chair, out of sight for a bit.

Maybe I should stop pouting about the HAMs being too little to play with me, because I'm going to need some time to get in shape before they're Lizzy and Abby's age.

But I'm up again and on the job as soon as the next crumb drops. All this to impress Granny by cleaning up after five kids.

Christmas presents were as follows: Hunter got his first Tonka truck. Maxwell got a helicopter he can pull with a string. Ava got a baby doll that giggles. And there was even a stocking for me with a new hairbrush and more dental bones. *Awww Granny, that was sweet.*

Granny snapped this picture of our family and she called us the Lee Five. I wanted to say, "Hey Granny, don't forget me, it's the Lee Six." Sorry you were left at home in the basement, Riley.

Comment from Scotty the Scottish Terrier:

Lexi, you've accomplished a great thing for your family, finding a house! Give yourself a pat on the back!

I'm nine years old. Some would say I'm a senior citizen in human age, so you get the picture. I'm old. During those years, I've moved three times. Moving is hard for animals and their humans.

Your move sounds especially difficult since your Mom and Dad are working on a fixer-upper, moving in a short timeline, and selling the house in which you're currently living.

Be patient with your humans, Lexi. I'm convinced they won't leave you on the farm. They love you too much.

I'm sorry Christmas at Granny's house did not go quite as planned. Sounds like the farm woman likes to keep her animals outside. You're lucky to be let in at all, especially after you tinkled on her living room carpet. I don't think she could envision herself driving two hours with you in her passenger's seat.

JANUARY 15

http://lexitriplets.blogspot.com

We're here! We're home!

After weeks of preparation, I now sit in my new basement blogging to you—thank goodness my computer was still in the bottom drawer of the old desk— commemorating this important occasion in the life of my family. The Lee *Six* has moved!

Let me back up and fill you in on what's been happening over the past three weeks.

Gray Granny has been here helping Mom with the triplets on Tuesdays, Wednesdays and Thursdays. She and Mom continued to go to the new house everyday, coming home smelling like bleach and paint.

She'd go home on Thursday nights and then she and Papa drove back in Papa's pick-up truck on the weekends so Dad and Papa could deliver load after load of things we could do without to the new house, like an extra couch, boxes stored in the basement and stuff from the garage. We wouldn't need the lawnmower and weed-eater in January, but Dad said we'd better keep the snow shovel till moving day.

We repeated this routine for about three weeks.

Every night after the babies and Granny went to bed, Mom and Dad spent hours stuffing everything that wasn't nailed down into boxes then stacking them in the garage to be moved in the next load.

Last night, the night before the BIG move of all the important stuff and people and hopefully me, temperatures dipped and hovered around zero. Mom and Dad decided to make one last trip to the new house to drop off buns and sloppy joes for the movers the next day and to check to make sure the heat was on.

They left Granny, the HAMs, and me in the mostly-vacant house. Even the triplet table and almost everything for the babies, except their cribs and one small basket of toys, had been moved.

Granny and I had the job of feeding the babies and giving them bottles. Mom and Dad said they'd be home by bedtime.

Granny sat cross-legged on the floor in front of the babies who were propped in their soft Bumbo seats. She opened the three jars of babyfood--orange, green and yellow--and I sat at her right hand as she spooned away to Hunter, Ava, and Max. I licked up any extra that might drip on the floor, so Granny wouldn't slip on a slimy spot. You know she's not as limber as she was in her younger days. All I could think was *What in the world will I do if anything happens to Gray Granny and I have to take care of the triplets until Mom and Dad get home?*

After the babies finished slurping the slop she cleaned their hands and mouths. I was prepared to help, but she kept shooing me away. Next she made the bottles. All three babies were cranky.

Max was reverting to shrill-scream mode, so she knew she'd better get a bottle in his mouth fast.

But first she laid Ava Girl on a blanket and rolled a clean cloth diaper under Ava's chin to prop a bottle in her mouth.

Hunter was the least crabby, so she let him lie on a blanket on the floor for a while and stroked him with her toe, kind of like she pets me with her foot sometimes.

Well, the bottle trick lasted about 15 seconds for Ava and while she was screaming full blast the phone rang. It was Mom saying that Dad had gotten a flat tire. Wind chills were below zero and Dad was trying to change the tire in the bitter cold.

They told Granny she'd have to put the babies to bed by herself and they'd call back when they were on the road again.

Granny went pale. I sensed her panic. I knew I had to do something besides pace. So, I laid down between Ava and Hunter to make them look at me. If I lost their attention, I'd lick one and then the other, or roll over against them. Well, this made Hunter so happy that he started to make poopy pants.

One doesn't need to have my keen sense of smell to detect that stink.

Granny knew it too, and she said, "Thank you, Lexi, for helping me. You're a good girl."

She started petting me with her foot.

Soon, Max finished his bottle and Granny changed his pants and ran him up to his crib. She left me on guard with Ava and Hunter.

When she returned, Ava was still fussing and Granny held the remainder of her bottle so she could finish it, then changed her diaper and took her up to bed.

By the time we changed Hunter's diaper, he'd waited almost an hour with pants full of poopoo, but he sure did enjoy his warm bottle as a reward.

I walked up the stairs with Granny when she put Hunter to bed. I leaned against her as we made our way downstairs.

When we got to the kitchen, Granny gave me an extra dental bone. *I never get two in one day.* As I ran to my pillow by the fireplace to savor the flavor she followed me. She sat on the floor beside me petting my head saying, "Thank you so much Lexi, for helping me. I couldn't have taken care of Hunter, Ava, and Max without you."

Then she flopped on the couch with a deep sigh and said, "C'mon let's snuggle."

I looked up at her. She was wearing that same pink sweater, the one from my nightmare. In disbelief I thought, *Did I hear her correctly? Is Granny really inviting me to cuddle with her on the couch?*

I was a little afraid she'd scold me, or maybe I'd heard her wrong, or she'd change her mind. But she scooted over to make room for me as she patted the couch cushion and I slowly slithered my way up beside her. Once I snuggled in, she scratched my ears and I think I heard her whisper, "I love you, Lexi." right before she started snoring. I didn't mind, I've been told I snore, too.

Before I drifted off, I pondered, *maybe Granny and I really are coming to love one another. After all, we love the same people, Mom, Dad, and the HAMs, and as a bonus we both love pink.*

Our snores synced and we kept each other warm until Mom and Dad finally came home, chilled and exhausted.

With the first light of day Papa arrived. Dad and Papa left to pick up the moving van. Then Papa drove Granny and the babies to the new house to get them out of the way as the moving crew of Grandma Strawberry and Grandpa plus friends arrived.

There wasn't room for me to go to the new house, and besides I had an important job to do here. I wasn't sure what that was, but at least I knew I had to bark like crazy as every box and piece of furniture was hoisted out the front door. Everyone shushed me and complained about tripping over me as I sniff-inspected every item.

Mom packed Riley in a kitty carrying bag

with a hole in one end where her head could stick out, kind of like a turtle peeks out of its shell. Papa didn't know what was in the bag, but could just feel something rolling around. When he tossed it into the truck, he said to Dad, "What's that, your bowling ball?"

Dad said, "No, that's Riley!" Papa picked the bag up again and peered in the hole to make sure Riley Cat was all right. She hissed back.

Many hours later, when everyone was sore and tired, the moving van was ready to pull out of the driveway to go to the new house to unload. Everyone was piling into cars. Dad's friend, I call him Uncle Matt, snapped this last picture of Mom and Dad at our little house. I'm not in the picture because I was shut behind the door.

Dad and Mom were ready to squeeze in the moving van--even the front seat was packed with computers and Dad's tech stuff.

They were about to lock the door and leave me until they returned tomorrow to continue moving the remainder of the stuff.

I couldn't believe the ingratitude! I worked my claws to the bone picking out this house for my family and I wasn't even going to get to spend the first night there?

I panicked and fumed.

I barked.

I howled.

I clawed.

Uncle Matt, said, "There's room in my car for Lexi." I took off before Mom and Dad could grab my collar and leapt into his car. Uncle Matt let me lie in the front seat on our drive to our new castle.

Winston, if you're reading, I apologize. I was so afraid that I was going to be left behind that I didn't bark good-bye to you, or give a farewell wave of my tail to my fenced-in yard, or the snow covered roses.

When we arrived I was ecstatic to finally see the home I'd chosen. There was the big yard I'd dreamt of playing in with my HAMs, the creek, and the woods. I wanted to leap out of Matt's car and just run and explore, hoping to catch a glimpse of my new neighbor, Marley, but Uncle Matt took me in and Mom and Dad put me in an upstairs bedroom.

After the truck was unloaded, Gray Granny took pity on me and put me on the leash to walk outside past Marley's house. After we returned inside family and friends filled their bellies with sandwiches and snacks as we all sat among boxes. I curled up on the couch beside Uncle Matt, listening to the laughter and baby squeals fill my house.

After everyone left, Mom and Dad were too busy to notice that I snuck to the basement to search for my computer in the drawer of the old desk.

Sitting here among the stacks of boxes, clicking away, writing to you all about our adventure, my heart flutters knowing *We're home. We're home. We're home.*

Comment from Peg the Pug:

Wow, Lexi, this is quite a post. You and Granny have both had a bout of panic.

You kept Granny calm when your mom and dad called about the flat. Yes, I know you were scared too; scared of what could happen if anything happened to Granny and you had to take care of the babies alone. But you pitched in and Granny sure appreciated it.

Great thinking to lay between Hunter and

Ava to entertain them.

I was astounded when Granny asked you to snuggle with her on the couch. I had to re-read that part because it was an unbelievable turn of events. Tears flowed.

I know it's been a confusing time for you, I've moved and also feared being left behind, however my experience was closer to Riley's. Mom stuffed me in my airplane travel bag, and the movers thought I was a duffle bag to be packed in the moving van. Good thing we were only moving about an hour away, or I could have been stuck in the back of that truck in my bag for an across country jaunt.

Blessings to you in your new house, Lexi. Thanks for sharing your journey with all of us. I feel like I know the other doggies who follow your blog. You've formed a canine network of support.

FEBRUARY 13

http://lexitriplets.blogspot.com

Lucky dog.

So, friends, let me tell you about our new house. We've lived here about a month. My office, the basement, looks about the same as moving day--boxes everywhere. There's just no time to go through things with Hunter, Ava, and Max on the move.

On top of it all, you can't believe the things the babies got for Christmas. Grandma Strawberry gave each a chair embroidered with their name. Ava's chair is, of course, pink. Hunter's is green, and Maxwell's is blue.

I've overheard Mom and Dad say that the former owners of our house used the front room for a fancy living room or parlor. This room now has a baby gate and is filled with oodles of toys.

"The playroom is for babies, not doggies."

Mom says. But, sometimes when no one is looking, and the gate is left open, I sneak in. A couple of days ago I stuffed both my froggy and my sock doggie in my mouth and laid them on the playroom floor. I wanted the HAMs to know that I have toys too, and I'm willing to share.

Without fail, Max, who moves the fastest, crawled to my toys, picked up my sock doggie, rolled over and stuck it in his mouth. (You know that's how babies learn, by licking and chewing everything.)

Granny was up to her elbows in Ava's diapering, when she heard the scuttle.

She squealed, "No, Max!" She quickly finished with Ava and laid her on the floor. Ava flipped over on her tummy, and both she and Hunter, crawled as fast as they could, almost racing Granny, to try to reach my froggy. The babies won.

Granny had to wrestle my toys from their mouths, then tossed them out of the playroom into the hallway.

Well, if the babies couldn't have my toys, they started after me pulling my hair. By then, Mom came to the rescue, and uncurled their clamped fists to extract my blond locks from their tight grip before they ate my hair. Then she released me from playroom prison.

That's what I get for trying to share. But, I suppose these are steps toward the babies growing big enough to play with me.

Sometimes in the quiet of naptime, I creep in and sit by the low windows so I can better perform my job as the castle guard, alert for approaching vehicles and pedestrians.

Flooded with light, the house faces east, so the morning sun beams through the windows in the front door and dining room. The back of the house faces west, so the last light of day streams through the kitchen and the TV room. If I've had a tough day, I can take a sunbath just by inching my naps from the front of the house to the back.

The crumb-droppers eat three meals a day now instead of just two, so my sanitation job has increased again by one third. After the HAMs finish their puréed combos of things like squash, spinach and pears, Mom fools them by pretending that Cheerios are dessert. She passes them out saying, "One for Hunter, one for Ava, one for Max, and one for Lexi."

Gray Granny continues her weekly trek to our house. She is catching on to my rules; for example, she often arrives with almost-empty peanut butter jars. She pets me, scratches me, Windexes my nose prints off the windows, and plays tug-of-war with my toys, but she continues to run that blasted vacuum every time she comes.

She and mom say my hair doesn't show as much in this house, it just spreads out more in a bigger space.

So, friends, the yard is beautiful with its creek on one side and the woods behind. I've seen cardinals, robins, and blue jays pecking at the winterberries on the trees. One morning four deer sauntered across the stream between Marley's house and my own.

A stray cat that Mom and Dad named "Coon Cat" stalks from the treeline, slinking through the yard, leaving her scent under the back porch, hunting to survive. She looks kind of like Riley, but bushier and certainly meaner. I'd like to chase her away. But, when I go outside I'm hooked on a very long leash secured to the porch post.

Since I'm new to the neighborhood and we have no fence, Mom and Dad don't want me to get lost by following my urges and my nose. This tether allows me access to almost the entire backyard, but when I try to lunge at Coon Cat, she slips just to the other side of the tree line, completely out of my reach.

I've overheard Mom and Dad talk about getting me an invisible fence by springtime so I can run and play in my yard. In the meantime I get in trouble because I'm impatient and bored, so I resort to digging and rolling under the porch trying to rid the yard of Coon Cat's smell.

Believe me, Mom and Dad are NOT happy when I come in the house all muddy and stinky, but they appreciate all I do and have taken me outside to play in the snow a couple of times, just the three of us.

Guess who romps free in the yard across the creek? It's Marley! We've barked back and forth.

She's welcomed me to the neighborhood and told me she's thankful for our blog communications, which led my family to this house.

Winston, I really do miss you. Has another nice doggie moved into my little castle?

Comments from Winston:

Hi Lexi. I miss you.

The new neighbor's trash is not nearly as good as yours.

Don't get me wrong. I'm so glad you found a new house for your family. They should be indebted to you, but they probably have no idea.

I'm happy to hear that you have more room inside. The yard, creek, and woods sound wonderful. I'm sorry you forfeited your fenced in yard with the pretty posies for a tether. Oh, the sacrifices we make for our humans.

Marley sounds like a nice friend. I hope you get to meet her soon. I feel kind of like I already know her because she's posted on your blog. I'd like to meet her in person some day.

There is a new dog in your place. She's small and looks like a dust mop. I hear them calling her Yorkie. We've sniffed through the fence. Even though she's tiny, she's mighty. Quite a yipper. I think they could attach a long handle to her and mop all the hair she must be dropping in your old house.

No worries that you could not say goodbye. Our friendship is not over, we'll stay in touch through your blog. Please keep me posted about your new life and your adventures with Hunter, Ava, and Max.

MARCH 12

http://lexitriplets.blogspot.com

Three Birthdays!

Tonight I write to you from my basement office filled to my shaggy ears with birthday cake and pride. My triplets, Hunter, Ava, and Maxwell had their first birthday today.

Mom decorated for the party using pictures of the babies from every week and month of their first year. The house overflowed with food, presents, people, and kids. The babies looked so cute in their Happy Birthday onesies.

The theme of the party was "tutus and

ties," so Mom had sewn little pink and purple tutus for the girls and little bow ties for the boys. Since I'm a girl, I got to wear a tutu also. Mine was pink.

Friends from the old neighborhood and family numbering about 40, played in the yard, and tripped over kids and toys in the house. One neighbor boy even brought *me* a present--a rawhide bone wrapped in birthday paper.

Considering it's early March, we had a gorgeous day, so Dad flipped burgers and forked hotdogs. Pasta salads, relishes, and fruit salads filled plates. With all the food spillage I had so much work to do to keep the floors clean.

Kids pulled my tail and ears, but I licked their hands clean in return. Adults tripped over my full figure, but I refused to divert my attention from herding my babies.

I rushed here and there to push wrapping paper, bows and tissue out of the way. These things are dangerous for my babies to put in their mouths.

Then came the big moment when the HAMs sat at their triplet table and each had their own little cake to smash.

Hunter's name was written in green on his cake. His hands dove in taking fistfuls and shoveling the sweetness into his mouth.

Maxwell's cake had blue icing. He poked at it with the index finger on his left hand. Once he'd made holes like a woodpecker, he used his pointer finger and pinched with his thumb to bring teeny tiny test bites to his mouth.

Ava seated in the middle, between her brothers, stared at her pink cake, but she seemed to be more interested in Maxwell's. Since he was eating so slowly she reached over to grab handfuls of his cake, leaving her pink cake unguarded.

Not to worry, Hunter reached over to Ava's

and began to demolish her cake with his heavy-equipment hands.

Once Ava realized her brother was pounding her own cake, she wiped her slimy, sticky, icing-covered hands through Hunter's hair and into his ear.

Her index finger brushed through Hunter's mouth and he clamped his teeth down hard. Oh, you can only imagine the shrieks from Ava, scaring the boys so much they started squalling too.

I was nearly out of breath, working like crazy to clean the floor by eating every morsel under the table, but the babies became so messy, I had to just start licking off their legs and toes and the fingers that hung over the edge of the table.

In between peals of laughter, our guests hollered, "Go, Hunter!" "You can do it Max!" and "Watch out, Ava."

I even heard someone say, "Good job with

the cleanup, Lexi!"

Thank goodness Mom and Dad made sure not to order chocolate cake, so I wouldn't get a tummy ache.

After everyone left, the house was a mess, but Mom and Dad didn't care, they scrubbed the triplets clean in the tub, dressed them in fuzzy warm sleepers and snuggled with them while they gave them their bedtime bottles.

I followed them up to the triplets bedroom as they plunked Hunter's pacifier in his mouth, laid Max on his tummy with his face on his softie, and turned on Ava's mobile. Mom and Dad leaned over the cribs; I sat in the middle of the room swaying while they sang

"Happy Birthday Hunter Bear,

Happy Birthday Ava Girl,

Happy Birthday Mighty Max,

We love you so much!"

So friends, as I look back on my life before the triplets, it was pretty good. But, even though my life changed within this year, and we've been through tough times, I love my babies and I can't wait to see what the next year holds.

And as a bonus now Granny even loves me.

I'm feeling dog-gone good!

Comment from Granny:

Lexi, I've found your blog!

I always knew you were one smart dog, but I'm astounded at your ability to rally canines, and problem solve together.

I'm sorry for any part I've played in your confusing year.

Yes, the house was crowded.

Yes, I was sometimes short with you because of your shedding.

Yes, all of my dogs have lived outdoors on our farm, so I'm unaccustomed to animals living indoors.

But, Lexi, I've come to realize you are special. You've not only accepted your responsibility of being a good doggie to Hunter, Ava, and Maxwell, but you've taken them on as your own litter. I couldn't be more proud of you.

I love you, Lexi.

ACKNOWLEDGMENTS

Thank you to Scott and Katie for letting Gray Granny invade.

Thank you to D.L. Stewart for believing I had a story to tell, and teaching me to write it well.

Thank you to the members of Medina County Writers' Critique Club for your acceptance, input, and years of encouragement.

Thank you to the many colleagues, friends, and family members who took time to read and give the gift of honest reactions to *Lexi's Triplets* in its early stages.

Thank you to Diane Cleavenger and her fourth graders at Black River Education Center for being enthusiastic beta readers.

Thank you to my husband who lets me work at home in the woods writing stories about our grandchildren and their doggies.

Thank you, readers. If you enjoyed this story about Lexi and her triplets, I'd be grateful for any kind words you might leave in a review on Amazon.

ABOUT THE AUTHOR

Jean Lee lives with her husband in small-town Ohio, twenty minutes from anything. She is retired after twenty-two years of teaching elementary school. Her children are married with children of their own. Five grandchildren are her greatest blessings.

You may contact Jean and Lexi by email:

lexitriplets@gmail.com

@LexiTriplet on Twitter

lexitriplets.blogspot.com

Her latest books, *Lexi's Triplets*, and *Lexi's Litter of Three* feature her triplet grandchildren, written through the voice of Lexi Lee, the family dog.

Her current writing project is *Julia's Journey To Her Forever Home*, written through the voice of Julia Noall, a Jack Russell Terrier mix, Lexi's cousin.